Sakura in the Gravity

Audrius Razma

"Only our children will know the truth."

-The Real Man

Sakura in the Gravity

Three friends one night in Japan receive a text message from an unknown number offering money for killing Yakuza; their journey of friendship in a military drama begins.

Their fight for life and friendship does take in a lot of places to champion their enemies they never intended to see or know about and save the world they live in.

Table of Contents

Takeshi Castle

When a business dealer does not pay what he owes, the business comes to a stop.

Welcome to the Northern European mind games from the depths of hell in business he was travelling.

The bodyguard escorted him home from Sweden.

The business dealer, he was a very poor reputation company director.

He was looking for very serious security. When he abused a woman and child, he knew the death threats he had were not threats of compiled letters.

The escort to Klaipeda was on a route through Latvia in a rental car to cross the borders to his mansion of sedition and abuse of power to a poor family.

His driver felt worn off from a long journey home, and it was late night they drove past near Nemirseta forest of the NATO Military facility.

When in the back, they broke their headlight.

The vehicles came to a halt exchanging their insurance details, and the business dealer stepped out with his bodyguard.

He squeezed his eyebrows, thinking those fools can escape without paying double to waste his time on a cold late night.

"This will cost you a lot more and you know it".

The first slug made its way in a bad business dealer's face leaves him to die.

Another gun fire round makes its way to the bodyguard's chest. With a hole in his body, he takes a chance for his life in the forest.

Our gunman with his six-shooter let his breath out.

"Why do you always have to get the right thing before the righteousness gets undone?"

He drove off, and it was never his intent to kill besides the target. He took money and pride to see laying corpse waste before his eyes.

* *
.

A little later, two school children are meeting their senior school friend in the cafe opposite the school.

He is now a fresh recruit to Lithuanian police officers.

His name is Simon Says.

He was a well-known rascal of the school. His graduating changed his views and to be the respectful guy in the ministry of justice.

Lord Ignacius and Magnum Mage who are young and open-minded schoolboys are now thrilled to meet their friend that led them through their junior years in their school.

"I know you just joined the police, but did you hear about the homicide? It took place last week, about a few kilometres away from our town."

"We have plenty of rumours, but nothing confirmed yet."

Magnum Mage stirs his tea and takes a sharp look, not taking his gaze off Simon Says sitting in uniform looking at two highschool friends.

"We will see what death will bring."

0.0

The days have gone and years followed within the days to once more for three friends to meet, but far from where they have grown up.

Downtown Osaka is full of bars and cafes overcrowded with a huge number of tourists from all over the world.

It is usual Simon Says has a bit of coffee and with relief of his breath thinking about his friends he speaks.

"If I would not have to run my mouth so far. I would not have to travel so far from home but I am happy to meet all of you again."

Mage leaning on his right arm places three fingers to his cheek bones to think more of Simon.

"I was always interested in other cultures. I never knew I would explore such an amazing culture with my friends. This is a double bonus."

Ignacius lifts his lips to smile and brushes his long beard before he replies.

"I am not that thrilled working here. I am a noodle chef but I was way happy to gain qualification after such failed school exams. You know guys from my experience, such a country we are in pays a lot more but at the end of the day I am left with a bowl of noodles on my table."

"We were a grand country before the Soviet war criminals. They ruined our economy with their military occupation and threatened everyone with their death camps."

Magnum Mage thought out loud from their school history books theory lessons they thought they knew.

"Simon, how is your life after getting caught for taking bribes and in police prison?"

Simon replies he is working for a private security agency that is built of a failed policeman like him.

"I enjoy once again providing safety to people and placing handcuffs on the wicked ones."

"I am just working in the farmhouse of my uncle. I cannot see any future besides this work."

Magnum Mage was not sympathetic answering his question and did not make eye contact just had another drink from his matcha bowl.

^.^

Our three friends walked to the district of the bars in Osaka.

When they thought they had enough drinks.

Ignacius' mobile phone flashes with a message from an unknown number.

The text message was written he has to reply yes or no for an offer of thirty millions of US dollars for a contract.

he replies yes.

Ignacius says looks to his drunk friends,

"I think you cannot believe it, but I said yes to an offer of ten million dollars from an unknown message."

"You are joking with me."

Simon pours another drink in his mouth.

Mage abstains from further comments. He is looking with them concern at concern.

When a second message appears in Ignacius' phone with instructions of how they should commit the hit to a local businessman.

Ignacius slams his drink to a table, spoiling his clothes with alcohol, finding it hard to speak out loud himself, keeping it long what he waited to speak long ago.

"Fock it I am going for it even to see if it is a joke because I dislike how locals treat me."

Simon cannot control his joy from a joke he thought to be in and found himself amused about his friends together and he felt a revolt he did in school.

"As a former policeman I advise you against your wishes."

Three friends take a walk out onto the narrow footpath leading from Osaka Castle hill holding onto each other.

The Botched Job

A man walks to a video games venue to see a well-dressed man in a tailors suit.

"Kitsuen wa anata o korosu koto ga dekiru koto o shitte imasu ka? (Do you know that smoking can kill you?)"

He offers a foreign man cigarette.

"Sukidesu ka? (Do you like one?)"

Lord Ignacius grins a smile from cheekbone teeth to teeth.

"Kore ga anata no hai o hiki hagasu koto ni chūi shite kudasai(Watch out for this will rip your lungs out).

Ignacius stabs through tailors suit in his heart with a chopstick, kicks him off his cutlery and rolls kicking dead leaving him be with a bag of rubbish.

Our white Mage is taking a walk along the river talking with Simon.

"What we are going to do if they know Karate?"

Simon slides his arm under his black denim jacket to reach the back of his belt.

"I will go like Indiana Jones and waste no time."

They continued the journey along the river to kill and earn their living.

When Mage and Simon approached the backdoor of the games venue, the lights sparked into the night with slugs entering bodies of men in black suits to see these men dying on the concrete floor with Simon holding his handgun.

They choose to carry on walking without waiting for them to die stepping over diseased like they were left there.

"Dude, where you got this gun from?"

Simon Says is looking at his piece of metal twisting in his palm examining and admiring the equipment he did hold in his left arm.

"I think officers are required to carry firearms."

Magnum shook his head and thought they are making a mistake drinking and believed the luck will come their way.

"I do not think you are an officer anymore."

Our heroes continue walking the building part made of offices to see if the path is clear and hoping to see Ignacius waiting for them at the very end of the destination to kill.

"What would you do if you run out of ammunition?"

"Mage, the gun is heavy."

He smacks two guys over their heads while they jumped out of the corner running outside to see what has happened in the entrances on the lower floor.

"Simon, I am confused. Why you did not shoot those two?"

Simon run out of those bullets and knew the handgun handle is a great tool to break car windows in accidents while he was in past patrol duties to see road accidents.

"This mister Smith and miss Wesson is a heavy coupe allowing me with the other end to knock out cold anyone who opposes their marriage."

Simon did make a journey to the top floor a lot shorter with Mage he gets a gun pointed into his forehead while one of the security guards are talking to him, presumably alert about events, he not knew to be true they made their way in breaking past building security that happed on outside.

He is asking them questions Simon and Magnum do not understand a word they are speaking, they chose to show rather tell their tale.

Simon knows what he should do and gives no break to others taking one step forward and twisting both hands backwards with the guard's firearm back at his jaw making his hand fire into his head.

The blood splatters a little onto their heads while the remaining mass of blood and meat is coming out of the victim's head onto a floor while Simon gently places him onto the floor.

Our Mage was looking behind him how he made it happen a lot easier than he thought to take one man's life it was easy for his eyes to see it.

"I think you could have him leave out cold like the other two guys rather than getting on us the blood splatters and cause loud noise in here."

"I got it covered, we are alive so far and let's keep it this way. Let's keep ongoing because I need to get paid."

Ignacius after dealing with a random guy outside the venue walks along with the coin-operated games machines into the backdoor as instructions said but he is feeling happy Simon said they will get the backdoor covered from outside in case it was a trap.

Who knows if the unknown number will pay so much it might be right for him to think he is safe. T

The trio is still drunk and in normal circumstances, they would swing around the place, but from so much adrenaline into the moment they could not care less.

When he got closer to the main corridor leading the aim got a great idea of how he could finish the job and is running perspective of success in his head.

He hears men walking fast, and a gunshot fired near to where he is lurking.

Ignacius picks up a fire extinguisher and prepares to see if he would need it in case his friends are in trouble.

"Mage, I think we need to stop talking because we are like letting them know we are here and we going to hurt them."

"Like we would not have done this already."

Ignacius swings this big canister for fire equipment learning Simon places his face into the wall.

"Guys, it's me!"

Simon lets go of Ignacius twisted wrist tilting his top shoulders in the art deco wall.

"I know, but I still hate when friends are swinging at me very heavy objects."

Mage thinks of silent treatment they should keep it their focus if they like to stay alive.

"Here goes silence treatment in a corridor."

When they walked a few meters further they have reached their eventual destination and while walking they run a thorough course of action.

Ignacius knocks on the door where is written the Kitaro Hiroshima the founder of Hiroshima Innovations and Developments.

Ignacius opens Hiroshima's office door a little wider to let his head out to speak.

"Jinsokuna ranmen no haitatsu (the speedy egg noodles delivery)."

The half-asleep man in the executive's chair opens one of his eyes to see three men in the next few seconds to tie him up to his chair and shut his sock into his mouth.

Ignacius does ask his teams for tips on how they should proceed with the homicide they are hoping to earn their living.

"What to do next?"

Simon's funny ideas did make humour much open he slides his arm in his backpack and takes out paper masks of geisha faces printed on them.

While three of them are wearing their face masks Simon did took leadership explaining the initiative to explain what he learned about contract killing from a professional police officer's career.

"I have a good idea how to let the contractor know about our job well done."

He takes out a mobile phone from Kitaro pocket and turns on YouBube application on the mobile saying to his friends on the quest there is nothing more interesting than watching YouBube live.

He places the footage to show a live media stream, Ignacius pulls out his mince clever inside his backpack of kitchen tools he carries to work and offers the struggling old man his last words.

"I said you will have the egg noodles."

He minces the target's testicles into nothing near to explain what a piece of meat it is, leaving him to bleed while he is on live video, letting our heroes have enough time to run far away as possible from the crime scene they just made for a promised pile of cash.

They hey left and are walking far from the town feeling drunk from alcohol and quite sick because adrenaline has worn off, Mage keeps thinking this will not go well.

* *

The epic night of the adventure having their night out is near an end, the boys are heading back to Ignacius apartment to sober up.

But Lord Ignacius eyes are captured to see shy pair of black eyes gazing at him and in a way saying hello to him.

With quick nonverbal communication, they join their hands together.

"Guys, you can head off without me. I think I am getting lucky tonight and I could use my private time."

Once a new couple is in Osaka Love Motel, Ignacius is taking his clothes off to see his lady is making her slow steps and licking her lips without taking her gaze off him.

But Ignacius grabs her arm and turns her around with his force.

She bends over to the table, leaving Ignacius holding her right arm with the blade she is holding.

Ignacius softly whispers like a tickle of the feather.

"Your blade or my stick up your backside because any of them can end up inside there."

He without speaking much to her do opens her up by ripping her stockings apart with the blade from her arm and ramps up himself into her backside.

When the time arrives for them to experience the moment of epic climax like a fresh couple, he cuts open her throat to let all of her blood sprays open all over the bedroom and then he remarks to himself.

"You should shut up your hole because I dislike talk a lot women."

He showers and goes outside to have a good smoke to learn he forgot his lighter.

Simon lights up his smoke not looking at him he says.

"You know this can be a bit of trouble for everybody."

"One or two now do not matter because this one was vicious. Also, I thought you guys have gone to bed by now."

"If you would have given us the keys you could have said that why we are here but otherwise, please keep it down. Ok?"

"This was the best minute in my life and I was hoping to marry her till death takes us apart, but death cannot make me happy."

"They all look dead to me when I look in their eyes."

Mage comments long far on the horizon not looking at his childhood friends expression understanding his thoughts.

"Ignacius, if you would like to find your genuine love then swap your TV channel and maybe then you experience better luck, rather than thinking everything is a video game while we are drunk!"

Our three friends are sobering up in an apartment in Osaka, the city is making a commotion from sounds of emergency services vehicles sirens.

* *
.

The sun is dusk near Japan, and two men are having a romantic affair with their hands on one another on a lovely evening.

One man closes his eye while another man places his tongue in his lover's mouth.

They finish their passionate kiss, then one of them goes down on his knees when another one lowers his pants and licking begins with kissing below.

He stands up from a tasteful mouth full of the passionate flavour in between the two, he unzips his trousers and turns round the strong sailor onto his stomach to show him how he is appreciating it.

^.^

In a post-war orphanage for children is in the north of Hokkaido, they are sheltering children who lost all of their families during the war, two boys were growing uptight as a fist and to find themselves to be the best friends looking into the world back at them to take it back.

One was Nobito and the other was Kitaro, Kitaro was later adopted in Hiroshima family when he was eight years old.

Nobito made his way into the world as he saw it fit.

Kitaro knew nothing but the love for a good street fight show everyone around who is the boss.

He was very brave and upheld his code of conduct while growing quick and strong into the cold post-war world.

.

When Nobito and Kitaro were sitting by the apple tree in Mae prefecture in the gardens of the apple farm. They left to see the farming community on their school trip from the orphanage.

"You know when I see apples on a tree it makes me think."

"What are you thinking about, Nobito?"

"Do all happy people grow up strong and healthy eating apples?"

"I am not sure if there is a happy people."

"I am sure we all can be happy."

"I feel happier already, and I find it funny to talk about it on such a sunny day."

"If you remember we learned from school mythology lessons about folklore from far away places talking about the meaning of apple."

"I cannot remember this lesson."

"Because you never listen."

The mile before he continues genuine-minded expresses his deepest desire to say it vocally expressing he says it.

"Because of apples are said we all must live lives of imperfection because we failed a test and fall far away from our apple tree."

"Does it mean those apples near us on the ground are like us."

Kitaro looks closer at an apple tree and the surrounding grass.

"What is the difference between those apples on the tree itself and the fallen ones."

"I think they are not different at all but the time got them to be a little different but if you think an apple can be on the branch forever it makes us fool for thinking like it."

"I know what are you saying but can it be it's just an appearance and I think any of them can be as good as on the ground or above, it's just a taste that differs from tree to tree itself."

"I agree."

0.0

Within, Kyoto somewhere on a sunny day a young man was enjoying the sunny afternoon all by him thinking how his time had gone by and how half-empty the time was.

It was late summer, but this time the weather was better than ever and he was getting ready to leave because his train back home is going to leave without him.

He was walking mindless and over-thinking, looking into the path where he is walking rather than around him. He accidentally walks into a girl with the impact makes both fall over.

Kitaro looks up and sees a girl who stumbled backwards, holding an empty fruit basket because he made her fall with all the fruits scattering around them.

He apologized and asked her name because he felt wrong for being so dumb.

"I am sorry for not seeing where I am walking because I am a little busy."

Her reply did make a choice the day they meet to find one another seeking a simple life they live to start learning it was never so simple.

"It is ok because I was so in a hurry to be back home I was careless. I am sorry too."

"Let me help you place those lost fruits back in the basket."

He was picking apples from the ground, Kitaro asked what is her name?

"My name is Sakura."

"My name is Kitaro."

He made it clear with a simple smile.

0.0

It was a day full of rain, a woman was walking in the Tokyo hotel district to meet the genuine passion and love of her life.

A little late lovers were finishing up their love affair, to hear a knock on their hotel suite door.

She opens the door to say she is a little busy, the handgun shell drops onto the floor making her fall backwards.

A man who was with her, while smoking his cigarette in the room's corner, says to the contract killer outside the door.

"I hope you do not think I pay you to make me drag her body into the bath?"

"No."

He closes the door behind him and takes dead Sakura by her legs, pulling her into the bathroom.

^.^

Our guys decide once they sober up to forget the night before they head out before a morning flight to shake off the stress.

The money did not arrive and no more messages about it.

"It's a great idea to go out for one more night together to a nightclub because I have work in the morning and I might not sleep well tonight knowing what we have done last night."

"Let's rock on tonight without a fail."

"I know one classy place for Osaka."

They come in a front night club on the front door written Royal Gigolos Nightlife and before they enter the nightclub Mage sends a text message to his grandad written 'EVERYTHING IS OK I AM COMING BACK HOME'.

When they enter the dance gallery on a massive marvel floor, the house music is playing and delayed flashlights are on the floor.

The DJ presents over the microphone about tonight playing DJ Benas Benosis, in the background starting the song, "when the truth comes out and all the joy dies, do you need somebody to love".

Mage looks around and says to his friends he is heading off to the bathroom have been holding it for a while.

Simon takes his drink from a glass bar looking around a marble floor night goes enjoying and dancing the night.

"Do not stay too long because it's my favourite remix playing now and I feel like going out for a dance."

While remixing "somebody in love" DJ is playing and disco flash is on the susceptible friends ordering their drinks and talking to each other the stranger slowly let his blade out of his sleeve and is walking up to them just to get his neck broken from behind to slide on a sofa.

The trouble does not stop there and there is further a man sitting by the table aiming the handgun with suspender just to receive ice pick into his ears and to lie down softly his head on his table.

When Mage comes out of the toilet and says to Ignacius he apologizes he took so long because the toilet was so messy.

The lights come on in the nightclub when the server screams she realises the blood is all over the table and the handgun is on the floor.

The lights come on, music shuts off and all the guests run for their lives out of the club.

Simon standing outside says to Ignacius it is a nightmare on an elm street did found its way inside the venue.

"It has never happened before, but I am sure they need to get some decent security outside the front door because it must be some kind of a psycho job in there."

Lord Ignacius replies clenching his fists irritated antagonizing way seeing his last night ruined with his childhood friends leaving far away home.

Mage does ask they start walking away because of coincidence it was a terrible mistake to stay around before they are noticed within crowds of witnesses near a murder scene.

"Let's keep on walking because we might get negative attention in particular after last night's heavy drinking."

Trio after a few more beers are walking closer to a central station to say goodbye to each other before they apart different ways once again, they think about getting a quick snack from the petrol station.

At the petrol station when they finish their snacks, Ignacius says he needs to use a toilet.

"I head off to the toilet; I hope it's not nasty as our previous place with all of those psycho killers inside."

He blinks at his friends and they return a smile.

Ignacius is using his loo, the man walks up to him and says something to him in Japanese.

Ignacius replies in his native language he is sorry he does not understand. But the man in the cleaners outfit grabs Ignacius on his collar and smacks him on the tiles, making him lose his consciousness. He drags Ignacius into the boot of the black car and then walks off.

Simon felt like he needs a toilet as well and walks towards the toilets when the black car passes him without stopping. When he walks into a restroom, he realises the blood marks on the floor and remembers the black car quickly leaving the petrol station.

Simon runs out when he comes to a situation to understand his childhood friend was abducted.

Mage walks up to him and says did Ignacius just pass out once again on his toilet seat.

"I have no time for this."

He rushes to the first vehicle left unattended and takes it to chase after the kidnappers.

Mage is looking at how Simon drives off with a passenger's van written on it "Korean Cheer Leaders" and is thinking to himself something is not adding up in here.

Simon is in such a hurry he does not notice the situation, he is driving a van full of fashion models who screamed while he is behind the wheel tackling in high speed the Kansai region tight bend roads to catch to another vehicle who have left about 8 minutes ago ahead of him.

The models scream and cry inside their van while Simon is steering the road; he plays the radio for a time being he would not take his sight off the road.

The radio is playing an Asian song in English, "Danger, oh my danger you're in a danger."

The girls in Simons van had enough and started vomiting, also releasing diarrhoea.

"I do like this tune." He increases volume and pulls all the windows open in the van.

He catches up to the vehicle of suspects, drives next to it and flashes his van headlights at them when waving them down with his hand.

Both vehicles come to a halt and the men step out of the black car for Simon to see them taking out of the back of the car crowbars and starting walking up to him.

"Great, what I should do in this shit right now."

The men stop walking up to a Simon in few meters away to listen to the humming noise coming in their direction on a side road.

Out in the forest under cover of darkness drives out a farm tractor driving all over them and not stopping heading back into the dark forest.

Simon looks at what he is seeing and what is left out of those big gangsters with crowbars thinking to himself.

"I am lucky enough I did not step out of this van."

Simon quickly runs up to the black car to make sure he chased the right vehicle to find his missing friend. When opens the boot of the car he sees Ignacius all in tapes and half-conscious.

Simon takes the tape off Ignacius's mouth and speaks to him to check his awareness and condition he is in.

" I came here in a hurry once I met all those hot models but do not go in a van yet to greet them because it's kind of awful smell ."

The Mage walks out of the dark forest and starts helping Simon to pull Ignacius out of the vehicle.

"What is next?"

"We need to drive quicker out of here because we have here the road of dead bodies."

"Apologies, I did not come back with the tractor because it took me a while to learn to use the breaks."

"Tell me about it."

"It was written in hiragana. I do not read Japanese."

"Great it was not written in katakana."

"I would prefer in Lithuanian."

"How about Eskimo?"

"What are you guys talking about."

They help him out of those silver duck tapes set his body free and off the boot to see him find it hard standing on his feet they help him sit on the edge of the boot looking at him in the eyes checking his vitals and observing him taking his breath finding his mind back to their normality they are found themselves in.

The trio boards a kidnapper's vehicle and starts driving anywhere they think can be better and further away as possible.

Fock Me Now Fujiyama

In the Kabuchi Strip club in Tokyo, two women are thinking about what customers are talking about when one replies she does not need to know but they need to keep their moneymakers moving.

Ignacius has a lap dance while is talking with Simon thinking about Hiroshima boss?

"Simon, I think if he is alive, I am sure he is a stand-up comedian by now."

Magnum sitting next to them is drinking water and thinking about the situation getting worse for them.

His friends are inside a strip club, the Bank of Hokkaido makes an international transfer to Orphanage in Siberia to the manager of the charity, Boris Blet.

He becomes curious about the transaction and makes a call to his secretary.

"Do you know why such a huge transfer was donated to us?"

"I am not, in particular, to know about this irregular transaction, but I can see they made before it."

"You can stop there, I will inquire myself from now on."

Three men done with their adventure in a strip club broke in a ramen shop above an old bicycle repair store and are whispering to each other.

"Lord Ignacius, it's not like we are stealing porn tapes."

Simon is helping Ignacius holding a flashlight for him to see what is inside a locker.

"Simon, I am not the one who will fill in a report about three armed thieves from upstairs who were heard laughing and used astral projection to transform into goats."

"Well, in here they can arrest only once."

Magnum standing in a dark corner is thinking how he could see their plan take further steps to avoid further criminal charges besides contract to kill, countless homicides and possession of firearms outside the burglary they are in process.

"Maybe we just leave a cardboard cutout of mister universe pointing out the window?"

But when Ignacius looks back he spoke in a light demeanour he would be sure they can be caught because they made so far leaving a trace of smoking gun they might end up dead before they reach the police station.

"Nope. We will later post them the photocopy of his bottom with a return label on it."

They felt amused and made no further talks laughing holding on their rib cages not to split from laughter vocal points out their lungs.

The next morning Simon was thinking why they had to go through all the problems to break into Ignacius the last workplace just to retrieve the blind man's walking stick.

"I wonder how big is Fujiyama?"

Ignacius opens his eyes because he was falling asleep.

"I think the hill is ok but I know a good place to stay with all the view you can manage from there."

When they reached the Fujiyama Prep School, two out of one was not even thinking about what they are going to do there.

"Home sweet home."

"Ignacius, are you serious?"

He is looking at the torn old rusty fence and the building looks like they abandoned it before they were born.

The green scenery made it look the nature took it back its place covering in and out in green leaves the branches of a plant coming out the broken windows and surrounding eastern side.

"I can feel a bad vibe coming from this house of terrors."

Their friend Magnum Mage made an observation, nearly walking over a bent school fence to see the building a little closer in the eye.

Ignacius jumps over the torn fence and turns back.

"Come on guys, I already posted our postcard to Hiroshima corporation!"

Then he turns to his school friends and walks closer to an abandoned building full of construction hazards.

A little later into the night Ignacius is taking the first watch in case they will become ambushed and Simon with Magnum is talking, looking into the night sky covered with stars.

"Simon, I heard stories they leave such buildings behind because they are full of evil spirits."

He is holding his breath in to avoid making too much noise when Mage smiles and turns his look to Simon.

"I wonder what kind of spook we find here?"

But when Simon replies the sound comes from above, like someone is in pain but very faint. However, Ignacius comes rushing in and holding his breath.

"Boys, I think we are coming outside because it's only one car just parked outside our school."

Trio friends go outside to meet their late hour visitors, they confront them and Magnum takes out his notepad and places it into his right palm before he tackles knife attack into his hardback notepad, retrieving the blade and stabbing the guy through his left palm blocking the knife go into his face.

Simon takes a large piece of wood and smashes it across the attacker's face, making him collapse, and a piece of wood goes into the guy's eye who was stabbed in the arm by Magnum.

Ignacius makes his run into the building, being followed by two men who are a lot larger than him. He runs up the stairs into the room he kept his night-watch and picks up the walking stick they had to break into his former job to take it back; he pulls the top of the wooden stick and now is holding a large silver blade. Then he circles two large guys who just run up the stairs and are losing their breaths making a large slash across one of them in the back and going for another floor hoping he will manage somehow. But when the guy comes up another floor level, he grabs Ignacius arm and gets hold of his making Ignacius arm break and let go of his weapon.

He takes his breath and with a second move, he uses the other hand to make Ignacius lose oxygen, slowly losing his strength. When suddenly comes a low voice from behind addresses the man who is about to take Ignacius life.

"Brother, what do you think you're doing?"

The man is at least two meters tall and wide shoulders built; peeking at them in the dark, making it hard to recognize his face. The strangler quickly turns around to throw damaged Ignacius body to the ground before he makes his run towards the man in the dark who interrupted him to kill Ignacius. The man in the dark does not flinch before he delivers a sudden blow to the killer, taking him by surprise and making him unable to talk or walk with half of his ribcage fractured in pieces. Ignacius takes his last look at the dark corner of the corridor.

"Why?"

But the man walks away yawning.

"I am Jack."

Magnum and Simon find their friend on the floor, they take the car left outside and head out of the area, realizing the plan they had was a pivot point of madness. When van from other sharp turn left flips them sideways on the road.

* *

Our friends are held captive inside the factory on the outskirts of Fukushima, the ice-cold water wakes them up chained to the floor in a shower.

Ignacius is feeling the pain of his broken arm and makes a scream from the pain of his broken arm in a chain.

Simon just takes a slow deep breath and says nothing when Mage opens his eyes, unable to see much yet from the heavy hit on his side of the car. "I think we might be done."

After a while, they unchain Mage from the heavy cuffs and take him across to another room behind the steel door. There is standing Boris and Kano looking on badly injured Mage's body and Boris says.

"This one focker is giving you a bad time and makes me a lot richer."

Kano smiles, lowers his face close to Mage and blows smoke of his cigarette right into Mage.

"I think I love them all since they saved us all a lot of trouble, he might be now my best friend."

He places his foot into Mages face, pressing harder and harder his skull against a concrete wall.

"Maybe you will be good enough to clean my shoes?" His laughing Boris reveals the truth behind their master plan.

"Well, I took care of your loose mother when you was focking her and now these idiots just smashed your dad balls because he was gay."

Our Mage uses his neck to push the sole. "What the fock?"

"Oh, you would like to know before you meet his daddy and mummy up above?"

Kano, "I would prefer not to embarrass myself to this shat eater, but I might let you have your fun Boris before I will make it quick. I give you ten minutes to find everything about them from this loser and finish it!"

They brought back Mage to the shower room to see his friends and placed him on his knees in front of Kano and Boris to see how they will react in a group because no matter how much they kicked Mage on a floor, he just was swearing and screaming.

Boris tells them to lower their heads and Kano asks his henchmen to leave the shower room beside Boris.

But Magnum looks with his swollen eyes to his classmates. "Do you remember when we were in school and we're watching the basketball games; we then were cheering from the tribunes above. We were making noise for our class in a game. We will rock you?"

Simon replies tilting his gaze to a side thinking it is the end letting vibrating reply out his frail chest.

"Sure, I was there too because it was a good way to skip lessons."

Magnum hits the hard floor with his knee twice and once with his shoulder into the wall but the Boris kicks him over into a corner.

"This one looks like he likes funny things! Should we shoot this kid right now or do you prefer to play a little longer?"

Kano rolls his eyes. "I do not care about those troublemakers, just kill them!"

Outside factory entrance stops a white van and inside a radio makes beeping sound followed by a man's voice ordering to all special preparation soldiers go to their work now.

The doors open outside the entrance to see who had parked outside their factory, a stun grenade falls the front door under the feet of Yakuzas, about to have a smoke. The live-fire opens from assault rifles pointing out the vehicle killing Yakuzas then three men step by step walks forward opening fire on their targets, wearing the flag jackets they shoot targets one by one.

Magnum smiles to himself on the floor and whispers three words. "Tik Tik Tok, we will rock you."

Boris turns his face towards the exit. "What a heck in a mother of god is these bulls noise coming from."

Kano takes his sixshooter from under his belt and aims to press the hammer at Magnum. "You die scum bag right now!"

However, the venture to pull the trigger was, Kano suddenly notices Boris dropping the floor with bleeding from his chest and forehead, Kano feels faint making him fall too with his body collapsing. His vision blurred dark with his body cold and numb.

The henchman suddenly enters to see his boss lifeless body on the floor and feel a sudden sharp pain in his neck when a knife from the back of his neck pierces his temple open and then turns to the side when it leaves his neck. He drops dead.

Outsider shows a hand gesture to follow him. Mage takes lead to follow the unknown male in black clothes holding CAR15 and P99.

Everyone is busy pointing their firearms in front of the factory, one guy is leading a rescue mission; firing rounds from the other side of the factory, closing the fire circle and killing all armed men, until he reaches his teammates and places hostages inside their transport.

The van is heading to an unknown destination and a driver is laughing and making jokes about how another guy picks a short straw to have hiked over the hills in full combat gear.

Simon felt uncomfortable about the rescue mission and made his mouth to talk in a black cotton bag.

"Who the fock are you guys?"

The Black Commando unit soldier is holding Simon smacks him over the head with his knee, leaving him to bleed from his nose.

But a driver stops laughing. "Come on, we should not treat our guests like this." With their van with our friends, above them is in air NATO, SS Spartacus cargo airship got intercepted by the Japanese ground control.

Their air defence ground operator made a signal to reach the incoming airship.

"This is Japanese military air space asking to identify yourself."

SS Spartacus made a brief reply to have one in return before it let its wheels out in preparation to land.

"This is Scandinavia 101, the strangers in the night."

"We have now the ground lights on, you are safe to land."

A little later and NATO SS Spartacus is refuelling when the van drives to Fukushima military air force gates without making a stop at the checkpoint they carry on driving into the back of a military cargo aeroplane and the Nato SS Spartacus takes off into the night.

Bags come off inside the van to the lucky trio who had a lot to go through. Then from a corner in the van comes a strong smoke, and a voice speaks to them.

"Hello, my name is Mark and be thankful to NATO Commando just saved your stupid heads in this shat hole."

"I would rather like to ask you why we here?"

"Lord Ignacius because I had officer's distress signal from NATO's Private Security unit and heard about you guys leaving a trail of smoking guns all over the island. I think you guys are funny and talented murdering psychopaths who would like to work for me since you know about us."

"I think three of us had enough of problems and we would like just to be home to forget all about it."

"Simon, I am Mark Ta and I am Vice General, a pleasure to meet both of you."

Simon takes his look in a light bulb moment to Magnum Mage and looks him in eyes.

"So you were the murderer on the dance floor?"

The Dolls House

Three friends were having their bowl of soup for lunch and thinking about their plans in Bangkok, Don Meung.

The place is an open-air tent with a trail of ants walking across the table into a bowl of sugar. The sunshine is making the sidewalk look all melting and portraying a desert mirage.

The plan was to make it a holiday before their true journey will challenge their friendship.

They were wearing matching shirts and black denim shorts. The black shirts in white palm tree print.

His head felt the sorrow of sweat on his forehead.

"I do not understand when I had to solute a poodle when we landed in Thai airbase."

"Simon, you know after everything we had to go through, I still believe we had to strap on dildos to surprise yakuza in Fujiyama elementary."

"I do not understand what are you guys talking about sometimes." Their Captain Mage did not care to know the details of their past adventures. Magnum Mage looked forward to the bowl of rice and seafood soup. It was sweet as milk.

"Well, I got lucky with brother Jack."

"What was this poodle they framed on gold canvas?" Simon thinks a little longer, making a pause.

"You have a Brother you did not tell us?" Captain Mage kept his finger on the spoon, keeping it twisting in his hand, looking to a lady in the kitchen mixing herbs and vegetables.

"You got me wrong. It was the guy who saved me in the ghost house. He sounded like Australian, therefore I call him brother."

"I see now." Simon pours a little water and thinks a bit about the place he is in, saying to himself why they serve hot soup on a burning hot day, making him drink all this water is driving him crazy.

"Do you guys remember the game plan Mark Ta has told us?" Their captain noticed the soup coming to their table.

"Yep, we need to find a lost kid on one side of the peninsula and bring him home before we all a fried up, we can do what it takes because if we end up dead we go to hell including millions of lost lives with our failure." Simon stretches his fingers together pulling them in one hand out to let his wrists rest.

Lord Ignacius sets his feet forward under the table to relax his shoulders before their meal arrives.

"Kop-Kun-Krap. Is he so stupid to ask us to do it?" Their meal arrives, and Lord Ignacius appreciates it.

"I am not guaranteed, but it is the job they drew us to now." Magnum Mage picks up between his fingers a silver spoon.

The very moment a drunk guy walks in making a scene, he is VIP taking a girl by the hand pulling her down towards the street.

"Ignacius, what are you going to do because of all the troubles on the loose?" Simon asked him, placing in his mouth all the boiled vegetables and white meat in.

"Let's eat first before we go, otherwise we stay empty stomach." Their captain made well in a good hope intended observation, mixing his rice and white meat to set soy sauce flow.

This said Ignacius stands up and pushes his chair in a way of the couple leaving the scene.

The VIP guy is furious at Ignacius and says to him he should leave.

"Mate, you should had mind your own dam business."

"Me sorry me no englesse!"

Lord Ignacius grabs the chair smacking a guy in the head, takes him by his collar, places his neck on the chair's leg and breaks his neck for good.

All the three NATO heroes make a stroll down the street to avoid attention from what just happened, but the girl approached them.

"Sawadee Krap, thank you saved me. My name is Pan Narak."

"You get better focking lost too or otherwise you sleep in a dumpster." Lord Ignacius just saved ran away.

"You should not be so harsh." Magnum slapped his shoulder in a quick snap, Lord Ignacius unable to see a twist of his arm fast than one second in his mind.

"I am sure she is a prostitute or worse because I just lay down her customer and she is looking so friendly looking for another customer." Lord Ignacius scratches his crotch.

"Here is our ride to our beach resort, let's get in before we become a local sensation."

Simon shows them a fist to the air crossing his left arm punching his right fist walking away letting them know he is no fool.

Our heroes in the night meeting point at a bar. They had all afternoon to catch some sun on their skins.

But one guy and he sat at a reserved table next to a palm tree waving to our three friends. He calls himself El Paso. "Hi Hibler!"

"A? Do you have problems with us?" Simon takes a seat closer to him.

El Paso relaxes his shoulders in the chair he is sitting in and moves his lips to each ear cheek.

"Guys, after our active fire standard training I have not seen you, rookies!"

"I was happy enough to know it." He orders a waitress to pour a drink in.

Paso does show two fingers in the air and licks his lips. "I heard you guys are going on a top-secret mission to save the world, it's so confidential you cannot share it on Fokbook? "

"You know Facebook is just communist malware but for free?" Simon made a joke-cracking their rib cages and all laughed before they ordered their drinks.

Our diamond formation heroes are enjoying their pineapple juice and rum, smoking the Cuban cigars El Paso had brought them from Cuba.

"This is a proper Cuban missile crisis here I am holding." Simon draws his mind to closer inspection of burning tobacco leaf held three years in before it leaves to customers.

"You never win against communists." Simon's communism joke made their minds rest at ease before they entered the combat project NATO Vice-General assigned.

"I was long before you two working on these projects when I met Magnum, he was a shy kid before we thought him ways of murder, but most creepy enough is he is a still shy kid."

Once El Paso said, making others smile except Mage.

"Tell me about it, today we run into a shy couple with one guy getting all talk a lot with me before he ends up ill." Lord Ignacius scratches his hair.

"You know this makes me think Mage is not a creep here, he accepts what it is with his heavy heart but knowing how you play all happy and cool when you bend all these fools. I think I should double lock my bedroom while you are around." El Paso drops ash of cigar in an ashtray.

"I know and we had to share the same bunk beds while we had prep training?"

Simon exhaled his cigar smoke.

"We are childhood friends and we are in NATO-like one unit."

He makes another smoke to let his dark smoke fumes fill the beach night air fill air.

Our Mage was gazing into the stars before he had another drink and then all left to sleep since they all had plans.

^.^

They had enough drinking and Ignacius ends up in a royal kickboxing stadium taking a fight to amateur winners stadium in the blue corner.

To see suddenly lights go out and come back on with a loud microphone.

"Can you smell what the debt is cooking?"

Then from the podium to run in two guys wearing spandex shorts and spandex masks.

.

The mage had a good last drink to stay at the seashore to see his friends heading out.

Simon makes a call a little later, about Ignacius taking a walk by himself and knowing about the early flight tomorrow morning.

He heads out to the last location he went missing.

They are asking around at the bar they saw him learn he was talking about amateurs fight he was very interested in.

When they head towards the stadium El Paso taps Mage on his shoulder to tell him to look above into a fog light to see Ignacius' face across the other guy.

The voice in a stadium announces the debut of a new fighter, the Cowboy versus the Big Bulldog, to start in the next half an hour.

They look at each other and say together.

"I think we are all in for a fight now."

The commentator shouts it will be a spectacular night watching this fight: Lithuania vs Georgia!

Mage heads to the TV operator's room giving a light knock on the door to hit the cable guy on his face with the same door he opens.

He walks in and pulls the guy's arms in closing doors behind him.

Our Magnum shuts off all communication lines and runs an ID caller block blocking a few kilometres of all mobile lines off to give some time for them to take Ignacius back.

When the lights shut off, Simon and Paso put on the spandex suits and looked at each other.

Simon adjusts his mask.

"I hope we never do this again."

El Paso does show his genuine smile.

"No worries, our love affair is only between us."

The guys run in a stadium waving at the spectators and heading towards the Big Bulldog holding lighters in their hands to increase their fist blow power.

Simon jumps over ropes takes with him a folding chair and gives a good throw at Ignacius, making him fall down the floor already from weak legs after over a limit of alcohol in his blood flow.

El Paso runs up to the Black Bulldog and smacks him over the floor but he pulls back the ropes blocking his face expecting another blow.

Our El sidekicks him a few times into his ribs, causing his ribs to break and fall onto the floor from the pain he has.

He does not stop and picks the Big Bulldog by his legs kicking him into a groin shouting.

"How do you feel now Mr Big Bull?"

Simon helps Ignacius grab Paso on his sides.

"You should stop, have you gone mad, we should leave now!"

Lord Ignacius does pull El Paso from the stadium floor, leaving the big bad Georgian Bull laying for the crowd to see him fail.

Then a commentator's voice appears announcing.

"We all know how we love American wrestling and we brought you this show and a surprise present. Hope you guys have a good night and applause to our lovely foreign actors."

The crowd gives applause, and Mage once he finishes with the announcement shuts off the stadium lights.

A NATO team runs to the street where Mage is waiting outside the emergency exit with a random car he unlocked from his mobile IT device and waves at three guys running out in long coats. "Do you guys expect it to rain tonight?"

Simon takes off his spandex mask.

"Nope. We were at the Royal Wrestling Stadium."

^.^

The morning of a flight on a TV channel in Thai local news the channel Thai BBD is running a news report in English about the Korean industrial revolution to avoid loss of commerce making more robots to handle the manufacturing industry.

When he notices the news headline, Ignacius does look to a TV drinking ice cold water to fix his health.

"It would be weird to see the machines go on low oil strike and turn the streets like in genesis movies, protesting with blasters against police officers."

Simon walks by to a showroom. "I would not go to work then."

Mage pays no attention to the media on TV.

"The world is changing and those who probably cannot adopt are on a news channel."

They later are heading to a bus stop for the airport, Ignacius does go across the street from a bus stop saying to wait for him while he buys some water.

He walks on zebra crossing to learn that in Thailand zebra crossing does not allow you to have a right to pass the road first.

The vehicle does not stop on a pedestrian line and Ignacius instead jumps away; he jumps on the front of the vehicle when the vehicle runs away with our hero.

Ignacius smashes open the windshield with the driver's face when he places his arm in through the side window and grabs the driver's collar.

He gives a finishing blow to cave in the window into a vehicle and gives him access to the car.

Our Ignacius gets in while on the road and punches the driver's head until the vehicle turns off the road and flips over.

Ignacius pulls out the driver and continues to kick and punch him.

The car pulls over with Mage and Simon, they whistle Ignacius and El Paso behind the wheel.

"I thought you guys might use a ride to this flight?"

The tall guy who was watching the road rage is looking at those assailants driving off and making a smile with waving hands while they drive by him.

A Thai girl walks up to him and kisses him on the check.

"How are you today, Ban Toya?"

Toya looks at her.

"Blat, you won't believe what I just witnessed, Pan Narak."

.

The Mage is sitting in an A16 seat on his flight to Seoul and takes his travel sickness pill to help him have some sleep after a long night.

His eyes are closing, he watches how Simon and Ignacius are already asleep.

Mage suddenly wakes up to the feeling.

He is in Ignacius' body but he is old and sitting in a wheelchair.

The good-looking nurse takes him into a garden and she is smiling.

She then parks him in front of the flower bed, then she smiles and waves to gardeners.

The men wave back and she walks to them, she hugs one and kisses the other one while she is still holding one's private part.

They all smile and laugh sitting on the bench covered by trees but directly under Ignacius' view, Mage can sense how Ignacius feels angry all boiling inside his body but unable to flinch.

The Japanese nurse spread her leg over one guy's leg, giving him access to his finger to go inside her bottom, while the other one is kissing and touching her bare breasts.

The guy pulls his pants down and starts pressing down on her on the park bench.

Mage suddenly feels gravity and is pulled into a space tunnel to travel in time.

He appears in Simon's body, having his eyes closed and feeling like he is kissing.

The body opens his eyes and he can see Ignacius' mother in front of him and a mirror behind he can see Simon's face.

The space tunnel pulls him out again, making him travel across the space once more.

He is now in his own body but he finds out he is a space pirate and the crew captain too.

He is on a mission to other planets to help his crew find riches. Mage travels into a planet of women where they promise a good life; they feed his men; they bed his men and they feed themselves on his men to find out the woman wants his men's soul to hatch the golden eggs.

Magnum rounds up surviving men and heads down into a cave as their revenge to break the golden eggs cave.

He then feels the ground is shaking and lights turn dark for him to open his eyes to see the plane is preparing for landing and he just woke up from having a dream.

The sunny days are in the past arriving at the passport point.

They handle their passports when they enter the checkpoint and when they had left, the passport officer thought to herself.

"Alfa Scheuffer, Tango Ventura and Bravo Dutch; how are strange these Lithuanian's names?"

^.*

Once the team arrived at the location, they left their bags at accommodation in Gangnam sixth-floor apartment and left for lunch to see how life is here and implement the orientation plans of trace and rescue.

"We are now normal tourists from Bavaria, we always add yayaya or ahh when we speak."

Mage is walking and thinking about their future.

"Ya ya ya."

Simon practises his vocal cords.

Ignacius adds his voice. "Ahh."

Our team was heading to the local cafe for a quick shot of coffee and a sandwich when a stranger was looking at them from a building window across the street.

The cafe staff were in a good mood and one guy behind a till was holding an interest in his customers.

He stayed close and joined the table of theirs to learn about customer service first impressions.

"Hi guys, I hope you speak English. I am Bibi Bit. I am happy you like our cafe place."

Simon does appreciate his cafe.

"I wonder if he intends to sit here long before we leave."

He lifts his finger on a coffee cup looking out the window. He places his arm back on the sofa chair and relaxes his feet.

Mage appreciates the hospitality.

"We could use local guide intel about anything we might now know."

Ignacius sits closer to him.

"We could take on subcontractors too."

Bibi Bit smiles and moves his eyes to his fresh interest.

Simon looks back from looking at the window across the street.

"We have one extra teammate on the way since there are four formations in the guidebook?"

Ignacius drinks from a cup of coffee.

"You do not tell me he is the guy who made us a coffee?"

Mage drinks coffee too. "I think he makes excellent coffee. Let me ask you about the time you complete your work and head out to see the nightlife."

They had a full lunch. The phantom was still looking at them outside his window when Bibi Bit did ask how the meal was.

Simon left an extra tip in Won.

"Ya ya we understand how important it is to the hospitality business to provide excellent customer care and we would love to have your time if you don't mind?"

Bit made a small sudden bow.

"How could I help you?" He sits closer and listens intensely.

Mage does make a proposal asking for help.

"Ahh, we are new here and a little worried about nightlife hidden dangers and we would be happy to ask you to have us to show you around and as an extra job."

Ignacius takes out his envelope of cash.

"How about 500000 won for a three day's tour guide after work, ya?"

Bit smiles and starts thinking he could use a deposit to add for his new rent key money to rent his apartment.

Simon knows they need to start with local criminal gangs to find intel that is free of access to lead points, and he thinks about how he could take the point at the moment.

"How about a local place where we could treat you to serve you soup because it is cold here from our sunny place."

"Maybe I could ask you guys how I could spell your names?"

"I am Vlad Tango, this brown hair guy who doesn't speak much is Algimant Bravo and the guy with beard all over his smile is Pioter Romeo."

Simon gives his hand. "I am happy to know you."

"I am sure you guys are funny ones, I am happy to head out. I close the shop around 8 PM so come before then to have shots on the house before we head out."

Lord Ignacius brushes his beard hair.

Mage thanks and adds his hand too to a formal handshake.

Ignacius adds his hand too, turning into a team shake. He speaks.

"Fighting."

All let go of the handshake, the joy flows through their hearts.

They walk into the street, they know they made the first step to infiltrate the local community to look for a crime organization and find the lead to the hostage location before it is too late.

Their Captain made an important impression his team would never forget.

"I think we are now Littland Organized crime gang taking over the control."

Simon looks at him brushing his bald head.

"Do you think it is ok, how about our boss Jon Gi Sigis, you know he hired us from Japan?"

Ignacius understood Simon's improvisation did help his team.

"We will do well in a murder case from our last kill point."

They all smile to themselves while walking away laughing in their minds and repeating.

"Littland group hehehehe." They knew it was too important to fail.

^.^

They end up in a local food stool singing and overflowing soju shots one after another for Simon to see the group of funny guys in a suit with palm tree shirts telling the old lady off.

He stands up and says to his drunk friends he needs to take a leak. Simon walks around the back of the outdoor toilet to find a brick.

He walks up to a gangster looking guy to hit him over the back of his head with a brick.

Ignacius shows up from the other side walking to hit one with his shoulder.

It happens he slaps the guy over his face, making him hit the ground.

They finish kicking them all over the floor. They feel so bad they let one survivor go when he screams.

"I will take you to court for this."

Simon waves with a smile on his face. "You should tell this to the Littland Group."

They come back from a good fistfight to find Mage and Bit holding onto each other's shoulders pointing fingers at each other and saying to each other. "No, it was not you."

Mage stands up and looks at their teammates asking them how long they had to drink by themselves.

"Did you guys have to sock each other off for so long in a men's bathroom ya?"

"Ahh, you just look like you will not sleep alone tonight." Simon takes a seat back to the stool. He is feeling his feet are killing him.

"You guys start speaking English or this tour guy will go crazy." Bibi Bit points his misguided finger at Simon.

Simon opens an extra bottle of soju.

"Hey Bit, have you heard about the Littland crime group around here because we just had their feathers up."

"I never heard of those pricks, show me them and I beat them to a pulp for scaring our beloved tourists here."

"Ahh, then might I ask you who is the real villain around here in case I might run into them?" Lord Ignacius waves to bring more Soju.

"This Aisel Hasel Goon and his prick Sin On. They are always like on crime scenes and all over the news but never seen in prison."

"Ahh." Simon and Ignacius both pick Mage and Bit to head off to a taxi point to help them home.

Lord Ignacius pays the bill and takes a couple more bottles with him.

^.^

Mage walks into a kitchen to help himself with a cup of water for his headache and sees Bibi Bit laying on the floor.

He looks at Simon. "We are holding our team briefing today because our teammate has just landed and should be in an hour."

"No worries. I just quickly helped him to sober up because I think he will have some wonderful coffee once he shows up at work."

"OK."

"By the way, is it the best they had in a street league here abusing this grandmother for petty cash?"

"I do not know, but why did you guys make them scream like pigs nearly scaring me and our buddy Bit? I had to have a good few drinks together to make me forget about it."

"No worries."

"We should announce our fictional crime boss ASAP, about Jon Gi Sigis and his right-hand arm about Jon Sin. We need strong diversion because lawmakers and law administration units are not aware of our presence and won't until we all turn to ashes."

* *

A taxi arrives outside their apartment block for a young lady to walk out with a large grey hat and large brown coat holding silver hand luggage in her hand, making her way to three friends waving.

She stops, lowers her head. "Konnichi-wa, I am Sakura Uto."

Simon stands tall greeting her.

"Well, denim and leather have brought us all together."

Secta

Simon wakes up from hospital bed on the northern side of the peninsula border to see his teammates under oxygen and life support machines overseen by the Korean nurses.

He says to himself I cannot believe the dream.

"It was my late father taking me out of the darkness, his face was covered in scars and he was asking me to wake up."

"I can still hear his voice, wake up my son."

***

But before all chances come to light we can follow our heroes journey.

Before she managed to arrive Simon Says went to a gym center and inside he entered a martial arts dojo for his first free lesson. He changed to black tracksuit bottoms and white t-shirt; he thought good sweat will help him avoid a stronger hangover.

Then he did ask for extra lessons to test his skills further because the group was for beginners. When he was training in private sparring the dojo master hit him in his back with bamboo straw to help him fight further, "attack attack", but he beat them up and bent them over their heads for apology suddenly to learn he broke a straw stick in half and stuffed it on their backsides.

"Banzai!!!"

He was shouting and after he went out for a cigarette leaving his new sensei suffer in the dojo.

He drew on his hand three circles elongating the middle one.

"I think it will be perfect Ikigai to them."

Later he was in police custody while interrogated and was asked what it is, and he replied, "it is my dick I whip you with".

He jabbed the station officer down to the floor and grabbed the running sergeant by his collar to smash his head so hard into the wall his hat fell off.

Now he has them tied down on the floor, he starts kicking them and continues his investigation about the missing kid.

When Simon returns Ignacius asks him.

"How is their strong arm of the law?"

Simon drops his gym bag and before walks away he says, "They are still probably deeply in shat."

***

They welcome her into the Hansun apartment residency they rented for a couple days to complete the mission they were given.

She steps in the lift giving a shy smile to see Simon smiling full cheeks back. Ignacius winks at her and Mage keeps a close eye on her and then exchanges expressions.

They walk in through the apartment door and Simon says to her he will personally show her room so she could settle in as quickly as possible and while she puts the bags down, he would make her cup of black coffee.

When she walks away.

Mage is holding his mobile phone in hand looking at the message he just received.

Simon looks at him while he is boiling the kettle he says, "I would love to have one of those super phones but my budget cannot allow it", Mage "we keep minimal contacts with the boss therefore we keep limited connection devices in our team."

Simon, "What is good online for us to know?"

Mage sits down, closes the phone and leans his head back to close his eyes.

"There is nothing much in our network, it just reported that the BBD Brit secret service has gone missing after he decided to accept murder contract and kill one well known boxer. I think the agent 's name is Edward Hogson."

Simon pours in hot water for coffee to brew and places one cup close to Mage.

"I think I was watching the news the other day and they mention some sort of murder investigation."

Then Mage picks up the cup of coffee and starts walking to the end of the corridor, "I will take her coffee to her to see how she is doing and do not forget our codenames we only use because she has her own we do not know."

Simon, "Roger that and over or out", then he places his legs on the table and has his fifth cup of strong coffee today.

Mage walks up to her bedroom and gives a knock to her door, "Sakura-san it is Algimant-senpai and I am holding your coffee."

She opens her door, "arigato".

She uses her both hands to take coffee from him, "I would like to know where the washroom is because Vlad-senpai was so urgent I would see my bedroom. I was not able to know the apartment well."

He shows her around the penthouse suite apartment then he smiles.

"Apologies we were on low funds to have it with a swimming pool." She smiles too.

When she did have her hot shower, the guys were preparing a strategic team meeting and were completing data analysis of geographic and cultural objectives.

She walks in blue jeans white silk shirt and says she is happy to have the work done together.

"I am happy we can work together and I would like to be debriefed how much we are making progress in our case".

Team captain Mage looks across the living room dining table and says to her she could join a spare seat to join the data analysis.

"We have a belief it is an organised local crime syndicate responsible for kidnapping our target and they are believed to make an attempt to ask a ransom at a later date but we have no time left to conclude therefore we are made to act in such a quick way."

Sakura sits down and looks through Daily Bong newspapers archives the team had received from the data analysis team after their field Intel was complete.

"I see Aisel Hasel Goon and Sin On are the top suspects to be masterminds in the conflict to come."

Simon grabs a bit of his lunch sandwich and once he swallows with a cup of water, he takes another copy of the report they had received and pushes across the table to her.

"I think tonight we can raid their nightclub the Iron Quest to see if we can make vital intel points for us to complete on time."

Ignacius brushes his right arm across his brown beard.

"We are the Littland Organized Crime Group we have portrayed the other night and we should press the overseas mafia's attempts to have the race for control of the country."

Sakura looks to Ignacius, "How we proceed."

Ignacius, "we made clear the fictional crime boss and his henchman identity, for us to conclude Vlad is Jon Gi Sigis and Sin On is just a ghost to cause larger distortion."

Mage concludes the team meeting.

"Great, welcome to the northern European mind games, I hope you will like it."

Sakura stands up and makes a short bow.

"Arigato."

Mage suddenly stops to stand up.

"My apologies, I almost forgot our communication codenames because we use pseudonyms while we work but we will need open channel names. I was instructed to inform you I am Live Wire, Vlad is Torpedo, Pioter is The Streets and Sakura is Wildflower."

***

While the daybreak was near the end and night life slowly creeps in the day, the NBL special delivery courier pulls over the back door to deliver the package addressed to Sin On.

The delivery man walks out the driver seat to open the rear van door looking down at the floor and walks to the intercom to dial the doorbell call.

"I have a special delivery for mister Sin On therefore I would be happy to have him sign the parcel today."

Then couple minutes later you can hear the steps taken leading down from office above the ground floor storage gate when delivery man picks up the metal bar near waste container and breaks down security camera; then man opens quickly the door inside grey gates for Simon to spray in Sin On face.

"I hate bad breath", when man quickly collapses Simon throws in the parcel and pulls in Sin On inside the van to escape.

Mage parked the blue van near the district the team was taken to enjoy nightlife the previous day by their new acquaintance Bibi Bit.

"I think Sakura-san, you had a great strategy for us just to locate the important target rather than causing a mess and waste of time clearing their night club."

Sakura was sitting inside the van with Ignacius and was talking about planning and concluding the post-intel action plan how they could proceed the rescue when radio makes a spark and they can hear Simon.

"The Torpedo has completed it and is now heading towards The streets assembly plan."

When they hear a loud vibrating sound after they start their vehicle.

Simon starts his van in a hurry and when he runs the speeding vehicle down the corner he presses the remote inside his pocket to cause a large explosion from a parcel he threw inside the nightclub back gates.

When he stops in the outskirts of Seoul in an old abandoned road around the corner from the cargo container, he radios through to Mage.

"The Torpedo has delivered a patient to the care home."

Mage opens the door of the shipping container.

"The visiting tour has just started."

They open the van doors and cover his head with a coffee bean bag then they gently lift him out the van holding onto his arms and legs carrying him inside the container to place him onto a chair.

Sakura uses rope around his legs and finishes the knot around his waist.

Simon pulls out a small jab needle and injects it in his neck. Ignacius leans back at the side of the container and looks in the direction the sun is setting down.

"Do you think it will work?"

Simon places the lid back on the needle and takes it back into his pocket.

"I am sure it will work Pioter, do you remember when I passed out during our mountain trek training and the big boss brought me back to life with the same chemical to complete the last 10 kilometres run with 20 kilograms bags over our shoulder?"

When Sin On starts to move his head and increases his breathing.

Mage, without waiting a moment to see how he responds to adrenaline, pulls the bag over Sin On's head and shows him a picture of their mission target.

"Do you know this kid?"

Sin On opens one eye. "Why should I tell you anything!" Then Simon slaps him over his face. "I think you should learn manners before we make you speak."

Sin On takes a good look at Simon and spits on his shoe after Ignacius walks in. "I think we finished here, I just opened his mobile encryption and synchronised his GPS history data to conclude we are dealing with a kidnapper."

Sakura Uto without taking a second longer pulls out her small silver open and presses it twice open to stab Sin On in the neck.

Simon takes a look at her small clenched fist with a silver pen sticking out of it, "What a nice middle finger she has."

Mage start to take the ropes down and asks his team to help him to carry Sin On out the container.

They walk around the side of the container near a large hole they dig inside the ground, they place the Sin On unconscious on to the ground and Simon pushes him with his foot inside.

"I think you guys were doing a lot of labour while I was driving around the club district.".

Mage takes a shovel and starts to throw the soil back into the pit, Ignacius walks up the pile of rocks piled up right next to the shovel and picks one up.

Mage asks Ignacius to stop with the huge rock in his hand.

"We must wait before he has white foam out his mouth to know the black crab poison is effective."

The moment he says about the poison the moment white foam starts to float out Sin On's mouth but suddenly Ignacius throws the large rock on to his head making blood splatter over the ground.

Simon, "I was hoping you will not make me puke today Pioter".

Ignacius, "I just relieved his pain and misery although I know his nerves had gone numb three seconds after he had it but just in case."

Simon, "I think you have problems Pioter".

Mage, "No complaining and we all start pouring the soil back in."

When they finish with the shovels, they take off the overalls and place them in a bin bag, and then hop in their black SUV.

Mage, "I hope we all are happy with our nature sightseeing today?"

Simon, "Yay it was fun fact."

Sakura, "I named my weapon a little finger."

Simon, "I wonder how about us?"

Ignacius leans back in the leather passenger seat, "I would like to call my knife a War Saber."

Simon, "I know all about your walking stick saber."

He starts to laugh and before he finishes laughing Mage interrupts.

"I would call my handgun Daku, because I like to know I can carry at ease inside my jacket and I like it black."

Simon, "I would never think about naming a dead thing with the name but if you guys talk about the fighting spirit, I could have it named a Whistle."

Mage, "How would you justify it?"

Simon, "I think at the times when we did not have real technology, a police whistle was the only way to announce the crimes."

They start their Black SUV and drive off the bumpy ride across into a clear narrow road leading back to the capital.

When they park back at the Hansun Apartments Mage tells them, he will return the SUV and on the way back he will complete the report back to NATO Vice-Commander about today.

He steps out of his taxi and when walks in the apartment lounge he sits down in the one seat sofa, places his left arm at the wooden arm of the chair and comfortably places his spine in soft black leather.

He opens his mobile screen and sends a message in a dating app X-partner a message to girl.

"I think a lot about you and I made arrangements for us to go out on a date, my work is fine so far and I think I will finish on time for a meeting at the cinema in two days."

Then a message comes back to X-partner, "I am happy to hear from you. I look forward to our lovely evening together."

Then he stands up and walks towards the lift, he opens the lift door with the resident card and walks in pressing the top floor button.

He comes back everyone relaxing on the sofa in silence, with their eyes closed like they would seek meditation relief.

"I never thought you guys are doing group nirvana seeking."

Simon turns his head, "I never did but I just enjoy a moment of silence."

Mage walks into his bedroom and takes a fresh towel before he goes in a hot shower.

When they all had a good shower they were enjoying a cold bottle of water and relaxing in silence inside the living room on a large sofa.

Simon, "I think we know a very great tour operator around here."

The doorbell rings and when Ignacius opens the door Bibi Bit is standing outside smiling.

Ignacius asks him to wait for them to get ready in 30 minutes and they will meet across the street in residential gardens.

Simon walks in his room to look for a blue t-shirt with a grey shiny suit he bought from a street merchants tailor shop in Bangkok.

Mage puts on a grey t-shirt and brown slim linen suit and Ignacius pulls out his suitcase white t-shirt and soft cotton blue suit.

Sakura walks in her bedroom and changes to black silk underwear and bra. She looks for her grey cotton maxi dress, brown sandals and takes her black evening bag she is holding inside black pouch, her folding mobile, the top designer watch 'travel machine' and her flower scent perfume she sprays two times around her before she takes white band to place her hair together.

She takes a look in a mirror and is thinking she is cute already to go out with new friends.

When they close the apartment and take the elevator to the ground entrance into the hall Simon offers to give her his arm so she could feel comfortable walking out.

They walk through the lounge of the entrance with brown sofa chairs and silver marble floor through the facade of exotic flowers and through a glass entrance into the path leading across the car park in residential gardens.

About the Author

Audrius Razma was born in Lithuania post-soviet era, he finished school in England. He is half blooded Swedish-German and Lithuanian-Latvian.

He admires masters filmmakers Takeshi Kitano and Guy Richie. His research and analysis was learned from a design of a book to be found easily enjoyed like a silver screen movie ticket.

Audrius studied art and design from minimalism design masters, was working in a fine art gallery and travelled the world. He is a writer.

Our writer is part of the American cartel writers group and professional writers partner in crime.

He has been an author for three years and celebrates the day he started his second birthday on the first of September. His first time ever he started school, picked up his pen and published his first book in Hiroshima Office Press.

He lived in England twelve years and had independent studies to learn and develop a new form of art writing from analysis and research he made.

It was a great help from private tutor classes and group classrooms to adapt his art and design studies.

His childhood was full of adventure to write about and now what he can write. He decided to write about his weakest friends who receive immortality in his story and unstoppable weapons to be our NATO heroes in a landscape arc forcing evil to suffer the very first moment of our characters.

They are our real heroes, never dying fighting for justice.

He is now a Business Masters Postgraduate from Spanish Royal Business School, Students Council President and Hiroshima Office Press Editor-in-Chief.

His twelve year old boy is living in Okinawa, Japan with his wife. The first son was born on his author's birthday and we have another September "Kawaii Sensei".

The word "Sensei" or a Master can mean to be a doctor, teacher or author in Japan.

His last book he wrote was acknowledgement and dedication he placed a crucifix in a military drama sequel for him never to be forgotten the day his first child died from coronavirus vaccine.

Audrius Razma served in the British Army and has a silver Crucifix Award from Pope Franciscus in a diplomatic post for his work.

He believes in the Japanese Communist Party. He writes Christianity Bushido content.

The Hiroshima Office Press.

Legal Notice

It's an art of fiction never intended to be a resemblance of living but create an alternative reality parallel to our lives, helping us experience a sensation and entertainment of non-existing events.

If the coincidental information about fictitious forms of work comes into mind, they never intended it to mention neither living nor dead from reality.

The copyright is solely of the author or is otherwise stated. With any misuse of the information and creative works, one will be liable for its actions.